IT HAPPENED IN THE WHITE HOUSE

Extraordinary Tales from America's Most Famous Home

KATHLEEN KARR

ILLUSTRATED BY
PAUL MEISEL

HYPERION BOOKS FOR CHILDREN
NEW YORK

For Roger Smith, Sage of the Great Northwoods
—K.K.

Text copyright © 2000 by Kathleen Karr
Illustrations copyright © 2000 by Paul Meisel

First Edition
1 3 5 7 9 10 8 6 4 2
Printed in the United States of America.

Visit www.hyperionchildrensbooks.com

Library of Congress Cataloging-in-Publication Data
Karr, Kathleen.
It Happened in the White House: extraordinary tales from America's most famous home/Kathleen Karr; illustrated by Paul Meisel—1st ed.
p. cm.
Includes bibliographical references (p.106).
ISBN 0-7868-0369-X (tr)—ISBN 0-7868-2319-4 (lib.)—ISBN 0-7868-1560-4 (pbk.)
1. White House (Washington, D.C.)—Miscellanea—Juvenile literature. 2. Presidents—United States—Miscellanea—Juvenile literature. 3. Washington, D.C.—Buildings, structures, etc.—Miscellanea—Juvenile literature. I. Meisel, Paul. II. Title.
F204.W5K37 1999
975.3—dc21 99-12388

CONTENTS

I pray heaven to bestow the best of blessings on this house and all that shall hereafter inhabit it. May none but honest and wise men ever rule under this roof.

John Adams wrote these words on November 2, 1800, when he moved into the brand-new White House. They are now written on the fireplace mantel in the great State Dining Room.

Home Improvements

Washington City blazed with flames.

It was the night of August 24, 1814. British troops had spent a week marching overland from their fleet of ships harbored in Chesapeake Bay. They met little resistance from American soldiers during this campaign of the Second War of Independence, the War of 1812. In the young nation's capital they met no resistance at all. The city was deserted—or close enough. Anyone left was hiding behind shuttered windows, frightened to death. But they could peek through those shutters— and what they saw made their knees weak.

Down on Capitol Hill, Redcoats swarmed like ants around the Capitol Building. Inside, their hatchets chopped at the woodwork. Paintings were ripped from walls to make bonfires. Rocket powder was added and torched. The symbol of American democracy—and every building nearby—burned. It all burned till the sky was bright as day over the city. Then it was easy to watch the Redcoats marching up Pennsylvania Avenue like a parade. The soldiers stopped to torch the War Department building. Next they paused before the President's House.

White and gleaming in the flaming night, the mansion stood solid and proud before them. General Robert Ross held back his fire-happy troops.

"Officers will inspect the building first. We shall see how President Madison and his wife lived," he smiled, "before we finish off their American palace."

They lived well. The elegant State Dining Room table was set for forty. Fine china was surrounded by dishes laden with food. Dolley Madison had prepared a victory dinner for her husband and his guests before fleeing. The British officers ate everything. They toasted King George—and even James Madison—with the excellent wine. Then, stomachs full, they gave orders for the mansion's destruction.

Outside, the soldiers watched with satisfaction as hundreds of windows wept tears of fire. The President's House, the Executive Mansion, the White House of the United States of America, was burning to a shell.

Above the flames and smoke, thunder boomed in the sky louder than British cannons. Lightning cut through the hazy air. When rain fell like hailstones, the British ran in retreat.

President **George Washington** (1789–1797) hated New York, his first capital. He didn't think much of his "palace" there, either. The brick house had ceilings so low that he had to hunch over and remind people that he was a man of "a full six feet." The ceilings were so low that the ostrich feathers in the headdress of one of Lady Washington's guests caught on fire from a chandelier's candles.

Our first president wasn't comfortable in his second capital, Philadelphia, either. Washington missed his Mount Vernon home and the Virginia countryside. He just didn't like big cities.

What our country needed, he felt, was a brand-new capital. One that was built from scratch, midway between the bustling life of the North and the more relaxed South. Washington knew the perfect piece of land to build it on, too. It was not far from Mount Vernon, on softly rising hills above the Potomac River.

In 1790, Congress agreed with the first president. Maryland gave up a little land, and so did Virginia. The

District of Columbia was surveyed. Architects were hired to design the Capitol Building and a suitable residence for future presidents. This home was to be finished by the year 1800.

The house sparkled from the start. It was built of white Virginia sandstone that stood out from the brick and wooden houses of tiny Washington City. No one but the stonemasons had a chance to appreciate the natural color of the stone, though. Because its texture was porous, letting moisture through, the building was whitewashed from the beginning. It got its first coat of paint in 1798. It was given another coat almost every four years thereafter. When the walls were stripped in the 1980s, workmen found *forty-two* layers of paint on the building!

When President **John Adams** (1797–1801) arrived in the brand-new Washington City in November of 1800, a lovely Georgian-style mansion sat all by itself on Pennsylvania Avenue. It was called "Georgian" because it was built in the style of fine houses popular in England during the reigns of King George II (1727–1760) and George III (1760–1820) of Great Britain.

Adams moved in. But the roof wasn't quite finished. It leaked. Glass hadn't been placed in all the windows, so winds of an unusually cold winter swept through. Water had to be hauled from a half-mile away. There was not a single bathroom. There was only a three-seat *privy* (an outside toilet, or outhouse) in the back, near the workmen's rough sheds. The President's House was not kind to Adams and his family that winter.

When **Thomas Jefferson** (1801–1809) took residence after his inauguration, the President's House was still cold. Jefferson wandered around in his robe and comfortable old bedroom slippers. Horrified visiting dignitaries considered this an insult. Jefferson didn't care. He was more interested in deciding what to put in all those rooms. He lodged his secretary, William Clark, in the huge, empty East Room. After he had shipped Clark off to explore the Louisiana Purchase with Meriwether Lewis, he used the East Room to store the piles of prehistoric bones Lewis and Clark sent back to him from the West.

Slowly, the rooms were finished and filled with more than old bones. The rooms took on functions. The ground floor was used for kitchens, laundry, storage, and servants' quarters. The first floor was used for ceremonial purposes. The more comfortable second floor was divided into chambers for the family, and office space for the president. Each presidential family was given money from Congress to make changes in the decorations.

The inside of the great mansion became an ever-changing home. But the outside remained the same. Even war didn't alter the way the huge white house looked.

After President **James Madison** (1809–1817) and his

wife, Dolley, lost their home there in the War of 1812, it took almost four years to rebuild the inside of the President's House. The outside only needed a new roof and another coat of white paint to cover the smoke stains from the fire the British had set. (Underneath all those coats of paint, soot still mars the stone. A small section on the south side of the house is left unpainted, as a reminder.)

On New Year's Day 1818, President **James Monroe** (1817–1825) and his wife, Elizabeth, invited the citizens of Washington City to come and see the rebuilt mansion. People arrived in droves, dressed in their finery. President Monroe had been minister to France during the French Revolution. While there, he and Elizabeth had saved the Marquis de Lafayette's wife from the guillotine—and fallen in love with French furniture. The President's House was furnished extravagantly in the ornate and gilded new French mode. It was even whispered that some pieces had been liberated from the Palace of Versailles!

Nearly every president left his stamp upon the place:

John Quincy Adams (1825–1829) added a billiard table. He paid for this himself—a full $84.50. Congress still accused him of "corrupting the youth of the nation" by introducing gaming to the mansion. Perhaps in revenge, Adams refused to buy enough chairs to seat his guests when Congressmen came to call. They could jolly well stand in his presence.

Andrew Jackson (1829–1837) bought chairs. Lots of them. His guests wouldn't "be kept standing upon their legs as they do before kings and emperors, till they are so tired as scarcely to know whether they have legs to stand upon." He also installed the first plumbing in 1833. This included a pump to draw running water and a "bathing room" with coal fires to heat water.

Martin Van Buren (1837–1841) put in the first furnace for heating.

James Knox Polk (1845–1849) installed gas lights in 1848. Sarah, his wife, was cautious of the new scientific wonder. She made certain that one huge chandelier in the Blue Room was left with its original candles. Sarah was vindicated at their next big party. The gas lines failed. Hundreds of guests were left to stumble about in darkness—until Sarah had her chandelier's candles lit!

Millard Fillmore's (1850–1853) wife, Abigail, was a schoolteacher. She was horrified to learn the house held not even a Bible or dictionary, because each former president had taken his own books away with him. She organized the first official library, with lots of books by Charles Dickens. President Fillmore was more interested in the quality of the food, so he purchased a brand-new stove to eliminate cooking in open fireplaces. Bewildered by the huge, magnificent object, his cook promptly threatened to quit. Fillmore had to go to the Patent Office to study the mysteries of the stove's drafts and pulleys, then give lessons to the kitchen staff.

Andrew Johnson (1865–1869) bought a barber chair. He also installed a telegraph office next to the president's office. Now Johnson didn't have to walk to the War Department, as Lincoln had, to read the latest news.

His daughter, Martha Patterson, ran the White House while Mrs. Johnson was ill. She busied herself ridding the East Room furniture of bugs. She also waged war on the tobacco juice that had been freely spat upon floors and rugs. These indignities had occurred after Abraham Lincoln's death. While Mrs. Lincoln mourned upstairs, mobs thronged through the mansion, looking for mementos of their hero. An overwhelmed guard said that "the White House looked as if a regiment of rebel troops had been quartered there—with permission to forage."

After being given a personal demonstration by Alexander Graham Bell, **Rutherford B. Hayes** (1877–1881) acquired a telephone in 1878. Unfortunately, it was nearly worthless. So few people had phones, there was no one to call. (Today, more than twenty White House operators work around the clock to deal with citizens calling the president.)

Before his untimely assassination, **James Garfield** (1881) ordered an elevator for the use of his aging mother.

Benjamin Harrison (1889–1893) brought electricity to the White House in 1890. After electricians spent four months wiring the place, his whole family was afraid of getting shocked, so they refused to touch the light switches. Servants had to turn them on and off!

Franklin Delano Roosevelt (1933–1945) added a fire alarm system and a swimming pool. The fifty-foot, heated indoor pool was built in 1933. It cost almost $40,000 and was a gift of the nation. It was mostly paid for by pennies sent by children so Roosevelt could have the only exercise the results of polio allowed him.

Harry S Truman (1945–1953) acquired the first television sets. The Trumans didn't care for TV, but the Eisenhowers (1953–1961) loved it. Mamie Eisenhower rarely missed the afternoon soap opera *As the World Turns*. She and the president had their dinners served on TV trays so they could watch the tube while they ate.

John F. Kennedy (1961–1963) added a hot line to Moscow in 1963. Contrary to what movies have led us to believe, this was neither red nor a telephone. It was, in fact, a teletype machine.

Jimmy Carter (1977–1981) was interested in energy conservation and had solar panels installed on the White House roof. **Ronald Reagan** (1981–1989) had them removed.

The Executive Mansion, like any home, began to look shabby every few years. Its first major renovation was in 1901. **Theodore Roosevelt** (1901–1909) said it was too small for his large family. He had the West Wing built, and moved all the offices from the second floor into it. He also had most of the rooms torn apart to put in new floors, and paneling suitable for the display of his hunting trophies. Not surprisingly, all this work disturbed the unofficial White House rats. Families of them had been hiding in the walls since their original construction. The rats insisted on coming out. They brazenly stole food from the kitchen and horribly frightened anyone in their path.

Eventually, walls began to crack again. Ceilings looked shaky. "If it is as bad as you say," **Calvin Coolidge** (1923–1929) asked White House engineers in 1923, "why doesn't it fall down?"

It nearly did when **Harry S Truman** (1945–1953) moved into the White House. Truman figured he'd give the old place a chance, and had some fresh paint slapped on the walls. Then the leg of his favorite piano fell through the second floor. Truman fled to Blair House, across the street.

Four years and more than $5 million dollars later, Mr. Truman moved back. The White House had been entirely gutted and rebuilt. Bulldozers had chewed up the insides of the hallowed walls. A new foundation and steel framework had been built. Two more basement floors with bomb shelters had been added. But the outside hadn't been touched!

This is the White House we know today. Its stone walls are two hundred years old, though the inside is nearly brand-new.

So why is the White House called the White House?

When it was first built, the citizens of Washington City thought of it as "that white house," sometimes even as the "palace." Mostly they called it the "President's House." Later presidents felt that "Executive Mansion" sounded more refined. But the building kept getting a fresh coat of white paint over its stones every four years. Eventually more and more people just thought of it as the "White House." It took Theodore Roosevelt to make it official. In 1902 he had the address:

**WHITE HOUSE
WASHINGTON, D.C.**

printed on all his stationery. It's been the White House ever since.

And yet, there was one scary moment in our history when all that almost changed. On December 7, 1941, Pearl Harbor in Hawaii was attacked by the Japanese. Planes dropped bombs destroying nearly the entire U.S. Pacific fleet. Radio broadcasters announced the surprise strike, shocking all of America. The cry "Remember Pearl Harbor!" was heard everywhere. The United States found itself in the middle of World War II, whether it wanted to be there or not.

Only hours after he had learned the news, President Franklin D. Roosevelt called an architect into his office. He wanted plans made for the White House. New buildings must be erected on the South Lawn for war workers. The White House itself must be protected.

Soon the Army was digging up the lawns to build underground bomb shelters. Through the bitterly cold winter of 1942 new basements were gnawed into the frozen earth. This was all done very secretly behind a high board fence.

Next the Army decided that the White House must be painted in camouflage colors. Perhaps, even (gasp) *black*! The generals wanted the most famous building in our country disguised so that enemy airplanes could not find it and bomb it. This idea annoyed Mr. Roosevelt. He firmly refused to be intimidated, and the Army finally gave up its idea. All through the war the White House stood gleaming white and proud.

It still does.

ALL THE PRESIDENTS' DOGS

There was chaos in Martha Washington's kitchen.

"Vulcan!" The cook screamed and shook her wooden spoon at the intruder.

"Vulcan!" yelled Mrs. Washington.

She lunged for the enormous French hound, but he paid not a bit of attention. His bright eyes saw only one thing. It was the huge ham lusciously roasting over the open fire. The very ham being prepared for George Washington's dinner. In a flash Vulcan escaped out the door with the prize in his jaws. Racing like the furies across the yard, he zigzagged between servants tripping over themselves as they tried to tackle him. Vulcan's destination was soon in sight. With a great bound he was home free in his kennel, enjoying the spoils of his daring raid.

"Papa," Mrs. Washington addressed her husband that evening. "I hope you enjoy what remains of your dinner. Your favorite hound has stolen your ham!"

"Madam—" Washington snickered, then roared with laughter. "My dearest wife. I wish him health in it, for a finer dog was never born!"

Dogs and presidents go hand and paw throughout the history of our country. **George Washington** (1789–1797) was very proud of the pack of five French hounds sent across the ocean by his good friend from the American Revolution, the Marquis de Lafayette. Succeeding presidents were just as fond of their dogs. During the early nineteenth century it was common to see dogs of every description wandering about—even in the President's House—so not much was written about these animals. A dog had to be mighty unusual to get people to stop and take notice.

Bonin was an unusual animal. He and several other "sleeve dogs" arrived in Washington while **Franklin Pierce** (1853– 1857) was president. Bonin came from the Orient. In fact, he had sailed to America on Commodore Matthew

Perry's flotilla, which had just opened trade with Japan. Perry brought lots of other presents from Japan as well, but President Pierce only had eyes for Bonin. The dog was tiny; so tiny that he could sit on a saucer. He had a head like a bird, large popped eyes, and the body of a newborn puppy. Best of all, Bonin fit perfectly into pockets. He spent much of his diplomatic career traveling in high style in pockets around Washington, delighting all who saw him.

Warren G. Harding (1921–1923) had no children, so he lavished a lot of affection on his dog. Laddie Boy had his own valet for daily baths, his own chair to sit upon during cabinet meetings, and his own social calendar. This included his own birthday party. Neighborhood dogs were invited, and a cake made of layers of dog biscuits topped with icing was served. After his master's death, the Airedale's faithfulness was immortalized in song and sculpture.

Franklin D. Roosevelt (1933–1945) had polio as a young man. Because of this, he spent the last half of his life in a wheelchair. This happened years before people would speak openly of being handicapped. President Roosevelt was very anxious that Americans should think of him as capable and dynamic—both of which he was. Still, he couldn't go foxhunting with hounds as George Washington had. He needed a different kind of dog. The solution was Fala, a black Scottie. Fala was the right size and had the right personality to sit on the president's lap without appearing silly. Featured in newspapers, Fala became a national favorite, especially in World War II, when he became an honorary Army private by contributing a dollar to the war effort. After this, hundreds of thousands of dogs across the country joined the Army, too! When Roosevelt died shortly after beginning his fourth term as president, Fala even went to the funeral.

John F. Kennedy's (1961–1963) family came to the White House with a Welsh terrier called Charlie, then quickly added a German shepherd named Clipper. Once settled in, they acquired Shannon, an Irish cocker spaniel, and Wolf, a wolfhound, both presents from Ireland. And then came Pushinka.

Pushinka was a fuzzy Russian mongrel with a history. She was brought to the White House by Premier Nikita Khrushchev as a gift from the Russian people. During this period, the United States and the Soviet Union were playing a high-stakes game called the "Cold War." Each country was trying to beat the other in everything. The Russians had already won one round by sending the first satellite, called Sputnik, into space. Later they sent a dog, Laika, into orbit. She was known as the "Space Dog," and Pushinka was one of her offspring.

Pushinka became a very special dog around the White House—after she was checked by security officers to make certain she hid no secret spying devices. She lived on the ground floor of the White House with all the other dogs, and went to visit the president and his children every day. She also fell in love with Charlie the Welsh terrier. Soon after this, Pushinka became the mother of four puppies: Blackie, Butterfly, White Tip, and Streaker. President Kennedy called the puppies "pupkins." America's adopted daughter of the Space Dog became a genuine celebrity.

After John F. Kennedy was assassinated, the new president, **Lyndon B. Johnson** (1963–1969), moved his dogs into the White House. Johnson came from a ranch in Texas and loved beagles. His favorites were called Him and Her. Johnson was a big man and enjoyed horsing around with his pets. Once he even picked up Him by the ears in front of photographers. The picture was printed in newspapers all over the country and the president received many letters from people worried that he might be hurting his dogs. Though Johnson was sure he hadn't harmed Him, he promised not to do it again.

🏴 **Richard M. Nixon**'s (1969–1974) most famous dog was Checkers. He was a black-and-white cocker spaniel that helped Nixon win the vice presidency under President Dwight D. Eisenhower in 1952, when Nixon won voters' support by talking about the dog during a television election speech. But King Timahoe, an Irish setter, was the dog Nixon brought to the White House.

The most famous of all modern White House dogs lived with **George H. W. Bush** (1989–1993). Of course, this was Millie, Barbara Bush's springer spaniel—the first White House dog to "write" a book!

Though it's been mainly a dog's world, cats have lived in the White House. There was **Gerald Ford**'s (1974–1977) Shan, and Amy Carter's Siamese, Misty Malarkey Ying Yang. The black-and-white "First Cat"

Socks single-pawedly held down the fort at the White House for President **Bill Clinton** (1993–2001) until the adoption of Buddy, a chocolate Labrador.

Socks really belonged to Chelsea, Clinton's daughter.

Socks had his paws full, especially after the arrival of Buddy. He even had to share the book, *Dear Socks, Dear Buddy*, that first lady Hillary Rodham Clinton wrote. But he still met and welcomed the visitors who tour the White House each morning.

THE FIRST KIDS

It was a rainy day and the White House Gang was bored. They tramped through the mansion looking for action and finally settled in a vacant room. Sprawled on fancy chairs, they stared at nothing. Quentin Roosevelt's eyes finally focused on the portrait facing them.

"Hey, Charlie!"

Charlie Taft perked up. "You've got an idea?"

"You bet! Grab a sheet of paper from one of those books on the shelf."

Charlie noticed the painting that was riveting Quentin's attention. He grinned, then tore out blank pages for all the boys.

"Spitball time!" Quentin yelled. "First one to get Andy Jackson dead in the eye wins." They lined up chairs at the edge of the rug. They popped wads of paper into their mouths. They began chewing. Quentin was ready first. He usually was. "Watch this one!"

Taking careful aim, Quentin pitched his sticky missile at the picture. It landed well within the gilded frame, smack on President Andrew Jackson's chin.

"Five points!" Quentin crowed.

More spitballs flew fast and furiously. Soon Andrew Jackson's stern features were ringed by a halo. Then Charlie Taft hit Jackson's eye.

"Bully good!" The boys cheered and ran to inspect the coup.

"Old Jackson never looked better," they agreed.

"Still . . ." Quentin considered. His hand shot out to do a little rearranging. "I think he needs some decoration on his forehead. There. Stripes, like an Indian chief."

Charlie nudged Quentin aside. He moved two more spitballs. "And an earring on each lobe, like a pirate—"

"Boys!"

The gang jumped guiltily at the roar of outrage. Quentin's father, the president himself, stood in the doorway.

"What have you done to Andrew Jackson?" President Roosevelt didn't wait for an answer. "Clean up your mischief and meet me in my office. Immediately!"

Theodore Roosevelt held a kangaroo court for the infamous gang. Quentin's friends were banished from the White House for an entire week.

🏴 **Theodore Roosevelt** (1901–1909) was not known as a strong disciplinarian. The misdeeds of his six children generally went unpunished by him while they lived in the White House. With the historic portrait of Andrew Jackson, though, he had to take a stand.

Other presidential parents were equally lax with their offspring's antics. Maybe it was the fact that their parents were too busy to pay them much attention. Sometimes the first kids were lonely. And sometimes they got into mischief.

Four-year-old Susan Adams, the orphaned grand-
daughter of **John Adams** (1797–1801), was the first
child to live in the White House. She was miserable
because her father had just died. Then she caught
whooping cough in the freezing house. She had barely
recovered when her playmate Ann Black accidentally
broke her toy tea set. Susan had the Adams temper—
and the Adams memory. She bided her time till Ann's
next visit. Then, very carefully, very methodically,
Susan destroyed the porcelain head of Ann's doll.

🏴 **Abraham Lincoln** (1861–1865) followed the bachelor **James Buchanan** (1857–1861) in the White House, moving in with his wife and boys at the start of the Civil War. His oldest son, Robert, was away at college. Willie, ten, and Tad, seven, had a tutor who gave them lessons in the Oval Room on the second floor. Willie loved to learn and even wrote poetry. Tad had better things to do. Among those better things was setting up a lemonade stand in the entrance hall of the mansion. Visitors coming to see "Paw" had better buy a glass, or else.

Or else what? Tad was known to pull the beards of gentlemen he disliked. If he truly despised them, Tad's pet goat was allowed to use her horns judiciously. (Yes, his goat, Nanny, wandered freely through the White House. At times she was even found chewing her cud on Tad's bed!)

Tad and Willie had some good times before the winter of 1862. They made reconnaissance missions from the White House roof, spying out rebels with telescopes. They enacted bloody battles in the attic and on the lawn. They repeatedly court-martialed and executed a soldier doll.

Then Willie caught typhoid and died. President Lincoln was desolate. He buried himself in the war the Union was then losing. Mrs. Lincoln was devastated. She locked herself in her room for months, and would not even go to Willie's funeral. With no one to comfort him, Tad became a hellion.

Kind strangers sent presents to Tad. One of these was a turkey, Jack, who became his special pet. Tad fed Jack and watched him grow. One day the boy ran crying into his father's office. He'd just discovered that Jack was being fattened for Christmas dinner! Abraham Lincoln stopped everything to reach for a sheet of paper and write a special wartime pardon for the Christmas turkey:

If Jack is not a traitor he should not be shot.
A. Lincoln

Jack was spared and spent the remainder of his White House days wandering around the lawns, amusing visitors.

Lincoln tried to spend time with his son, but it was never enough for Tad. Lincoln could be amused when Tad sprayed Secretary of War Edwin M. Stanton with the water hose. He was not amused when Tad bombarded a Cabinet meeting with his toy cannon. Lincoln was even less amused when Tad flung a Confederate flag from a window while his father was reviewing Union troops directly below. Tad wasn't a Rebel—he just wanted attention.

Other White House kids just wanted a bed. When **Rutherford B. Hayes** (1877–1881) moved into the mansion he brought a large family with him. Nine-year-old Fanny and six-year-old Scott needed their own rooms. So did assorted relatives and Hayes's older son, Webb, who became his personal secretary. Seventeen-year-old

Ruddy could never find a place to sleep on his visits home from school. The White House was so crowded that he had to bed down in a bathtub!

Maybe that's why Ruddy turned into a prankster. When the Hayes family made a train trip west in 1880, Ruddy joined them. Every time the locomotive stopped, local folks would flock around the train carriage for autographs. Ruddy's mother, Lucy Hayes, was particularly in demand.

In one town she neared the point of collapse after signing her name so many times. She sighed with relief as the engine finally pulled from the station. Then Ruddy came running into the president's car. Grinning, he handed his mother an autograph album. Disguised by the crowd, he'd been passing it through her window. Mrs. Hayes had signed her name fifty-six times for her own son!

James A. Garfield (1881) settled his wife, mother, and five children in the White House in expectation of a comfortable four-year stay. A new tennis court was laid out on the lawn. The kids skipped off by themselves to the local school each morning.

The Garfields had been a close family, but in the White House it took the children twenty-two weeks to arrange to have breakfast together with their father! When Hal decided he was in love, it required over a month to schedule a private talk about the young lady with Papa Garfield. By that time Hal was so frustrated he had given up the idea of marrying the girl.

After Garfield was shot by a thwarted job seeker, the White House found itself virtually childless under **Chester A. Arthur** (1881–1885). Arthur did have three children, including a young daughter, Nellie. But Arthur was so upset by Garfield's assassination that he allowed not a single word to be printed about, or even a photo to be taken of any of, his children during these years.

Benjamin Harrison's (1889–1893) children were all grown, but he brought along to the White House the famous Baby McKee. This two-year-old grandson was a favorite of the president. Harrison rather enjoyed reporters fussing over the child who was said to be "forever crawling over the first page of the newspapers."

Baby McKee's press was so good that when **Grover Cleveland** (1885–1889; 1893–1897) returned for his second term with his brand-new wife, Frances, and daughter, Ruth, publicity became a problem.

Baby Ruth was taken for regular airings on the

White House grounds. Soon crowds began to gather whenever her nurse wheeled her outdoors. One day Mrs. Cleveland found the crowds snatching the baby from her nursemaid and passing her around like a plaything. Truly upset, the first lady made her husband close the White House gates. His police force was increased. Gossip spread that the Clevelands were hiding the baby because she was half-witted.

The very pregnant Mrs. Cleveland waited until she gave birth to her second daughter in the White House. (Esther became the only child of a president to be born there.) That accomplished, the first lady packed the family off to the safety of a more private estate in another neighborhood.

Theodore Roosevelt's (1901–1909) family didn't give a fig what people thought of them. They expected to enjoy the White House, and did. When the Roosevelts arrived, Alice was seventeen; Ted, fourteen; Kermit, twelve; Ethel, ten; Archie, seven; and Quentin, three. They grew up in the White House with a father who couldn't sit still—unless it was family story time. Then Teddy Roosevelt delighted his kids with fairy tales, ghost stories, and yarns about his adventures out West.

Roosevelt's children didn't like to sit still, either. They roller-skated around the shiny new parquet floors

of the East Room. They slid down the grand staircase on trays stolen from the pantry. They leapfrogged over the upholstered furniture. They negotiated long corridors on stilts. Quentin felt so bad when Archie was stuck in bed with the measles that he sneaked his own pony, Algonquin, upstairs in the elevator to cheer his brother!

Ethel was a tomboy from the moment she arrived. The first thing she did was to explore the White House from cellar to roof with Archie and Quentin. When they moved their inspection outdoors, the second thing she did was notice the lamplighter across the street in Lafayette Square. It was dusk, and he was scampering up and down his ladder to light the gas lamps. With a wink to her brothers, Ethel climbed the posts after the lamplighter, turning off each light. When her prank was discovered, poor Ethel was put in the charge of a governess.

Roosevelt was blessed with daughters who preferred to think for themselves. His eldest, Alice, sometimes carried this to extremes. She liked to shock friends by carrying her pet snake, Emily Spinach, around with her. She liked to jump into swimming pools fully clothed, or stand on her head in the middle of polite parties. She was impulsive and enjoyed making an effect. Her father was asked why he couldn't tame her. "I can do one of two things," Mr. Roosevelt answered. "I can be president of the United States or I can control Alice."

Despite her outrageous behavior, Alice Roosevelt was everyone's darling. Songs and colors ("Alice blue")

were named for her. Her parents gave her a huge White House wedding in 1906. Even at her reception she managed to make a statement. When the wedding cake was being cut too slowly for her taste, she borrowed a ceremonial sword and slashed through it herself!

When **William H. Taft** (1909–1913) took over the presidential reins from his friend Roosevelt, there was a certain amount of continuity. Young Charlie Taft had been a member in good standing of Quentin Roosevelt's White House Gang, after all. Charlie carried a copy of *Treasure Island* along to his father's inaugural ceremonies, just in case he got bored during the speeches. At home in the White House, Charlie amused himself by learning how to operate the telephone switchboard and taking over when its lone operator went to lunch. But things were a lot quieter without Quentin around.

The White House stayed quiet for a long time after the Roosevelts and Tafts. Grace and **Calvin Coolidge** (1923–1929) lost their sixteen-year-old son Calvin to blood poisoning in the summer of 1924. **Franklin D. Roosevelt**'s (1933–1945) hordes of grandchildren only came to visit. **Harry S Truman** (1945–1953) had his almost-grown-up daughter, Margaret (who spent her White House years locked in her room training her voice for a singing career).

The next first kids didn't arrive until **John F. Kennedy** (1961–1963) took office. Little Caroline and baby John-John Kennedy were greeted at the White House by a snowman built especially for them. When it snowed some more, their mother took them for horse-drawn sleigh rides across the South Lawn. As they got older, a small playground and tree house were built for the children there, too. Caroline even had her own nursery school up on the third floor of the mansion. Jacqueline Kennedy worried about the children becoming spoiled. Well she might, when their hamburgers were served on silver trays by butlers!

Jimmy Carter (1977–1981) brought his youngest child, Amy. Amy was only nine when she arrived, and wasn't particularly impressed. She spent most of her time with her nose tucked into a good Nancy Drew mystery. Even her Secret Service escort was nothing new. She'd had security guards while her father was governor of Georgia, too.

Amy was happy to have the guards once, though. In the summer of 1978 she was taken to see a pet show where one of the elephants escaped. It raced straight at her! One guard picked her up and lifted her over a fence. When the elephant crashed right through, another guard grabbed her back to safety.

Chelsea Clinton was equally well protected. Her father, **Bill Clinton** (1993–2001), made it known when his twelve-year-old arrived at the White House that she was to lead a normal life. No interviews with Chelsea would be granted. The media was given a very large *don't touch* message. Maybe this was because Chelsea burst into tears on election night in 1992 when she learned her father had won the presidency! Like other first kids before her, Chelsea Clinton learned to survive life in the White House. Some of the benefits included trips with her parents to exotic places such as China and Israel—yet also like any teenager, she was delighted and relieved to take off on her own for college life at Stanford University.

WHITE AS A GHOST

A faint odor of incense hovered in the air. The gas lights of the Red Room were dimmed, then extinguished. The only illumination came from the candelabra set on the table before the spiritual medium. Mrs. Nettie Colburn Maynard bowed her head before raising her eyes to those surrounding her.

"We have come here for a healing work." Her voice was gentle, dreamy. "Together we will contact those departed souls—great ones and loved ones, who surround us like a vast cloud."

She turned more businesslike. "The chain must be formed. Place both hands upon the table, please. Grasp the hands of your neighbors. You must remain touching. You must remain in communication, for the entire séance. Should any of you fail at this, my trance will be broken. All will be for naught."

She watched as Mrs. Lincoln gripped the hands of

her guests to either side; watched as the president him-self followed suit.

"I will complete the chain." The medium reached out from her armchair and clasped the last waiting hands. "Do not break the circle. Do not speak until I have summoned the spirits. Only then may you ask your questions."

Mrs. Maynard solemnly surveyed those watching her. "We are ready, then."

She blew out the two flickering candle flames. The room fell into total darkness.

"Hear me!" she intoned. "We are waiting with our griefs! Come to us!"

The medium sighed deeply and lapsed into silence.

The silence lasted for a long time. It lasted until Abraham Lincoln began to twitch with impatience. Only then did the tapping begin.

Tap, tap.

Tap-tap-tap-tap.

Members of the circle gasped. Were the taps coming from under the table? Were they coming from above? Mary Todd Lincoln cried out.

"A manifestation! Is it you, Willie? Tell me it is you, my darling boy!"

The taps turned into a steady rapping. The raps became frenzied. They were joined by the rattle of a tambourine.

"It is you! Praise heaven! And is little Eddie with you, too?"

The rapping climaxed, then settled. It changed into one sharp knock for "yes," two for "no," in answer to Mary Todd Lincoln's questions. Those questions flowed forth until her husband could accept them no longer. His voice boomed through the darkness.

"And is Napoleon there with you? And perhaps Lafayette, as well? I could stand with some advice on the direction of our current war."

The raps stopped.

"*Ooh!*" Mary Todd Lincoln raised her hands in frustration, breaking the circle. She shook her fists. "How *could* you disbelieve? You've spoiled everything, husband!"

Spiritualism is the belief that spirits of the dead can communicate with the living through a medium. The phenomenon was alive and well in Civil War Washington. The famous Fox sisters from upstate New York visited the city in the 1850s, setting the stage. They were the ones who had single-handedly invented "rapping." (Perhaps "single-toe-dly" would be closer to the truth. Years later, the sisters confessed that under their billowing skirts their clever toes could "rap" up a storm.)

The war made spiritualism blossom. By 1863 there was scarcely a family in the North or South who wasn't grieving for a lost husband or son. Payments made to hordes of mediums were a very small price to pay for "talking" to one's dearly departed. They were a small price for peace of mind.

Mary Todd Lincoln was no exception. She'd had a mental breakdown after Willie's death from typhoid. Next, her brother and several half-brothers were killed fighting for the Confederacy. Mrs. Lincoln needed all the comfort she could find.

She consulted Mrs. Maynard, a well-known local medium. She also consulted less reputable spiritualists, including "Lord" Colchester. He was a charming con man who made a small fortune preying on gullible ladies like Mrs. Lincoln before he was exposed as a fraud.

Mrs. Lincoln held as many as eight séances in the White House. She held others at the Lincolns' summer home. Obsessed by Willie's death, she truly believed that "a very slight veil separates us, from the 'loved & lost' . . . that though unseen by us, they are very near." She told her half-sister, "Willie lives. He comes to me every night and stands at the foot of the bed with the same sweet adorable smile he always has had. Little Eddie [the Lincolns' son who died in 1850 at age four] is sometimes with him."

Under the burden of such grief, it is small wonder that the White House is sometimes believed to be filled with more than presidents and their families. Ghosts are also said to wander its halls.

Ghostly sightings in the White House seem to have begun while spiritualism was at its height during the

Civil War. Mrs. Lincoln was the first observer, but later occupants followed.

Abigail Adams has the honor of being the oldest resident ghost. She had one of the finest minds of her time—male or female. And she was never shy about saying what was on that mind.

In 1776, Mrs. Adams wrote a letter to her husband when he was working on the Declaration of Independence. She asked him to "remember the ladies" while organizing the new government. She meant it was time for women to have a say in politics. Mr. Adams smiled and promptly forgot.

Mrs. Adams followed her husband, **John Adams** (1797–1801), to Washington City in November of 1800. In a letter to her sister she was quite candid about Washington and her new home:

"I arrived about one o'clock at this place known by the name of 'city,' and the name is all that you can call so! Surrounded with forests can you believe that wood is not to be had, because people cannot be found to cut and cart it! We have not the least fence, yard or other convenience and the great unfinished audience room I make a drying-room of, to hang the clothes in."

Abigail's laundry room was the largest in the White House and is now known as the East Room. Its walls had not yet been plastered. Its two fireplaces could not begin to ease the dampness or the winter chill. Abigail's bones ached with rheumatism. Still, the laundry had to be done.

It's not so surprising that many people have seen Abigail Adams's ghost passing through the locked doors of the East Room. Her arms are always outstretched, carrying a load of invisible laundry. When her frustrated spirit passes, it leaves the smell of harsh lye soap and damp clothing wafting through the air.

Not all White House ghosts are presidential material, or even belong to a presidential family. When the Redcoats raided Washington and burned the Executive Mansion in August 1814, apparently there was a casualty. The ghost of a British foot soldier occasionally stumbles through the place. He carries a burning torch and is intent on completing his mission. When last seen, he scared the wits out of a visiting couple. The abandoned soldier spent the entire night trying to set fire to their bed!

Dolley Madison's spirit is much kinder. During her husband **James Madison**'s (1809–1817) presidency, she was known as Queen Dolley, the hostess with the mostest. She was small, prettily plump, and enjoyed fine frocks from France—usually topping off her outfits with turbans sprouting exotic feathers.

Dolley Madison loved nothing better than a good party, and by all accounts was the most delightful and hospitable of souls. Dolley was the official hostess in the White House for widower Thomas Jefferson before James Madison was elected. After Mr. Madison's death in 1836, Dolley returned from their Virginia plantation to give **Andrew Jackson** (1829–1837) and the next widowed president, **Martin Van Buren** (1837–1841), the benefit of her social skills.

When the Washington social season was slow, Dolley would sit on the porch of her house on Lafayette Square, across from the White House, comfortably rocking in her chair and nodding to passersby. Her house still stands, and gentlemen still tip their hats to her rocking ghost.

Not that Dolley's spirit could ever be tied down to a rocking chair. Glimpses of Dolley Madison have also been seen in the White House garden and at the Octagon House down the street, where the Madisons took shelter after the burning of the White House.

The White House Rose Room, or Queen's Bedroom (so named because five queens have slept there), holds **Andrew Jackson**'s (1829–1837) bed. "Old Hickory" was brought up hard and was a tough customer in his day. As a child during the American Revolution he was captured by the British and marched to a prison camp. Later, he killed at least one man in duels over insults to his beloved wife, Rachel. In between, he decimated the British in the Battle of New Orleans and chased most of the Indians out of the South.

Jackson was tall and gaunt, with glittering blue eyes and hair like a pigeon's nest. His temper was volcanic. He wasn't the sort of person you'd want to meet in the middle of the night. But wild laughter has been heard coming from his old bedroom. Mrs. Lincoln claimed she heard him stomping around the halls, swearing. Others working in the Rose Room have felt a hand on the back of their chair, a frigid coldness, and the distinct sensation of someone staring at them with piercing intensity.

The strains of **Thomas Jefferson**'s (1801–1809) violin have been heard floating around the second floor Yellow Oval Room. ("My, my," Mrs. Lincoln said to a visiting friend, "how that Mr. Jefferson does play the violin!") **John Tyler** (1841–1845) has returned to whisper sweet words to his lovely twenty-year-old bride. Mrs. Cleveland moans in childbirth. But **Abraham Lincoln** (1861–1865) is by far the White House's most famous astral visitor.

One of Lincoln's favorite spots is the central window of the Oval Room. This is where he liked to stand and think, looking across the grounds to the river, and Virginia beyond.

Then, of course, there's the Lincoln Bedroom. It wasn't where he slept, but it *is* where he had his Cabinet Room and signed the Emancipation Proclamation. This is the current home of his famous rosewood bed. Mary Todd Lincoln special-ordered it for her husband—a full eight feet long and six feet wide to comfortably fit his great height. Most of the modern first kids have held pajama parties here, in hopes of meeting Mr. Lincoln personally. Amy Carter even consulted with a Ouija board. It's been reliably reported that these kids had sleepless nights—but only because the bed was so miserably uncomfortable!

Yet others did encounter Lincoln in or near the room. Theodore Roosevelt was visited by Lincoln's shambling, sad figure. Grace Coolidge saw him dressed in black, "with a stole draped across his shoulders to ward off the drafts and chills of Washington's night air." Eleanor Roosevelt often felt his presence.

Harry S Truman (1945–1953) was woken early one morning by two distinct knocks on the door of his bedroom. Peeking out, he felt a cold spot and heard footsteps trailing down the corridor. Queen Wilhelmina of the Netherlands fainted dead away after opening her bedroom door to find Lincoln's large frame blocking it.

Lincoln has been seen sitting on his bed, pulling up his boots. Winston Churchill never talked about it, but after a one-night stay, he refused to sleep in the Lincoln Bedroom ever again.

Strange sounds in the night. The rattling of chains. Chandeliers that sway and tinkle without a breeze. Mysterious cold spots.

Are these really signs of a haunted White House? Or are they the natural results of old walls and sagging ceilings? Maybe they're the natural results of intelligent people overusing their imaginations.

Why would a ghost choose to hang around the White House, anyway? As Harry S Truman put it, "Why they would want to come back here I could never understand . . . No man in his right mind would want to come here of his own accord."

Curious, Strange, and Weird—All Happened Here

Col. Thomas Meacham of western New York State owned one hundred and fifty cows. For five days he turned their milk into curd and piled it into an immense cheese hoop and press. When finished, the cheese was four feet in diameter and two feet deep, and it weighed 1,400 pounds. Colonel Meacham himself accompanied the cheese on the long journey to its fate. Forty-eight gray horses drew the wagon to Port Ontario. There it was shipped amid firing of cannon and cheering crowds. Drawing ovations along the entire length of its travels, it finally reached its destination: Washington City and the White House of President Andrew Jackson.

President Jackson set the gift cheese in his Entrance Hall and served it at his final party before leaving office in 1837. The occasion was in honor of George Washington's birthday. The people did come to honor the first president's memory, and to bid farewell to their beloved "Old Hickory," too. But as an eyewitness wrote, they mostly came to taste the monumental cheese:

"The multitude swarmed in. The Senate of the United States adjourned. Mr. Van Buren was there to eat cheese. Mr. Webster was there to eat cheese. The court, the fashion, the beauty of Washington, were all eating cheese. It was cheese, cheese, cheese. The whole atmosphere for half a mile around was infected with cheese."

The mammoth cheese was offered in front of a huge banner emblazoned with the likeness of Jackson, surrounded by an eagle and stars. All 1,400 pounds of it disappeared within two hours. After the ailing Andrew Jackson tottered back upstairs to his bed, crumbs of cheese lay everywhere. The White House reeked for weeks.

Many other odd things happened around the White House. They happened because our presidents and their families were real people. They didn't live only in history books.

John Quincy Adams (1825–1829) sneaked out of the White House before dawn, the way he usually did. He took his time strolling a mile down the marshy hill from the mansion. He liked to reach his favorite spot by the Potomac River just as the sun was rising in the east.

There, with a smile of anticipation, he began stripping. Off came his frock coat and stock. Off with the waistcoat, shirt, and shoes. Off with his trousers and smallclothes. Each item was neatly folded and stacked on the great flat boulder that Adams considered his private territory. The shoes always topped the pile, in case of a sudden wind.

Feeling gloriously free, John Quincy Adams dove into the cool water. The president was skinny-dipping in the Potomac River!

He splashed and cavorted like a child. Why not? The

entire river was his alone—until an imperious voice
floated over the water to him.

"Come here!"

Adams's head shot up as his legs sank. "I beg your
pardon?"

He squinted across the distance. It was a woman!
Well, an old woman. And she seemed to be sitting on *his*
rock. Atop *his* clothing!

The old woman settled her skirts more firmly upon
her perch. "I am Anne Royall. The newspaperwoman
who's been trying to see you. You hadn't the time, so I
thought I'd make some for you."

"But, madam—"

"No buts about it. I do not intend to remove myself
from your articles of dress until you talk."

The president couldn't very well trot back to the
White House without his clothing. Not with the sun
already up. He sighed and paddled closer to shore.
Submerged to the chin, Adams gave Anne Royall her
interview.

Did this meeting really happen? Gossip and Anne Royall claim it did. John Quincy Adams was too much of a gentleman, though, ever to refer to it in public or private. All that mattered to him was getting enough exercise so that he could diligently perform his duties.

John Quincy Adams enjoyed his private moments swimming in the river, but his successor, **Andrew Jackson** (1829–1837), loved horses. As a younger man, Jackson had even owned a racetrack outside of Nashville. Still fascinated by racing, he brought his favorite horses with him to the White House. At first they were kept in the mansion, right beneath the State Dining Room. When that became rather smelly, he had large stables built behind the house, smack in the middle of John Quincy Adams's gardens.

Although he still sat a horse like a warrior, Jackson did not personally ride his racing stock. For one thing, he was too big. Instead, he sent for most of his stable hands and jockeys—all slaves—from the Hermitage, his Tennessee plantation. The White House grounds became the gathering place for horse people and racing touts. Jackson himself rarely missed a meeting at the local race courses, which were even more popular than cockfighting in early Washington. And he always bet on the horses.

James A. Garfield (1881) had studied and taught Latin and Greek. He liked parlor tricks—and his favorite was an eye-opener. The president was ambidextrous, using his left hand as easily as his right. He loved to show off this ability. How did he choose to do this? Garfield would translate and write in Greek with his left hand while his right hand was busily jotting down the same words in Latin!

Theodore Roosevelt (1901–1909) was a natural sportsman and athlete, but he wasn't born that way. Young "Teedie" was sickly and asthmatic. His mother fretted for his survival, while his father gave him an ultimatum: "You have the mind, but you have not the body, and without the help of the body, the mind cannot go as far as it should. You must make your body."

Theodore Senior installed weights and gymnasium equipment in the family home. His son stubbornly struggled with them during New York City winters. In the summers he was sent off to the country, where he rode, boxed, and studied nature. By the time he became president, Theodore Roosevelt was a strong, boisterous man whom no one could stop.

Roosevelt felt cooped up in the White House. Constant lawn tennis wasn't enough. Neither was fencing, medicine ball, or boxing. Roosevelt staged wrestling matches in the elegant East Room between American wrestlers and Japanese judo artists. When none of this satisfied him, Roosevelt would go for a walk.

Walking for Roosevelt wasn't at all what it was for an average person. The president invented a new kind of walking, which he called an obstacle walk, but which was closer to the sport known today as orienteering.

Roosevelt would slyly invite his guests to promenade with him. Then he would march them into Rock Creek Park. In a form of "follow the leader," everyone had to traipse after the president. And the president only went in one direction: dead ahead. Over tree trunks, through brambles, directly across Rock Creek itself Roosevelt would tramp and wade. The French ambassador, who came in full dress to the White House on a courtesy call, nearly found himself with a heart attack before the end of one of Roosevelt's "walks"!

Woodrow Wilson (1913–1921) was so enthusiastic about golf that he had his golf balls painted black so he could drive them in winter over the snowy White House lawns. For entertainment during nasty weather, Wilson

had a screen set up in the East Room. With a projector and projectionist, it was turned into a movie theater. A permanent screening room was later built in the East

Wing, and today presidential families can request any movies they want to see. Margaret Truman watched *The Scarlet Pimpernel* sixteen times!

When **Dwight D. Eisenhower** (1953–1961) couldn't get away from the White House to fish or play golf, he took up oil painting. He gave all his friends "paint by number" kits and ordered them to start painting. The president never considered himself an artist, though. One day someone caught him cleaning off a still-wet canvas and beginning all over again. Ike merely commented that a painting "was no fun once it was done."

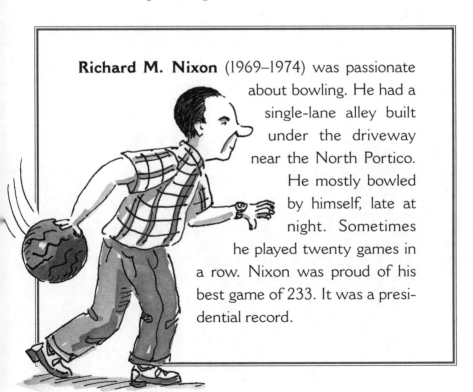

Richard M. Nixon (1969–1974) was passionate about bowling. He had a single-lane alley built under the driveway near the North Portico. He mostly bowled by himself, late at night. Sometimes he played twenty games in a row. Nixon was proud of his best game of 233. It was a presidential record.

Although considered one of the first conservationists, **Theodore Roosevelt** (1901–1909) was of mixed minds about animals. He loved them, yet he couldn't resist shooting them. During just one hunting trip in the Dakota Territory, he kept a neat daily tally of the animals he'd bagged: 170 creatures—including his first grizzly bear—all in forty-seven days!

His stay at the White House cut down his hunting time considerably. Still, he managed a bear-hunting trip to Mississippi early in his administration. When his party came across a bear cub in the woods, Roosevelt raised his rifle, took aim, then set it down again. Instead of shooting it, he picked up the cub and cuddled it. Reporters covering the trip took photographs of T.R.'s gesture. Before the year was out, the teddy bear was born.

The stuffed animals created a rage. Millions of the cuddly critters were sold. A popular board game, "Teddy's Bear Hunt Game," was invented. A syndicated cartoon, *The Roosevelt Bears*, arrived in the newspapers. Children could follow the adventures of two very Roosevelt-looking bears, Teddy-B ("for black or brown, or bright or bold") and Teddy-G ("for grizzly or gray, full of fun as a bear can be"), as they set out from the Wild West to take the East by storm.

Back home at the White House the Roosevelt kids were probably following the adventures of Teddy-B and Teddy-G when they weren't involved with the rest of their menagerie:

★ Tom Quartz and Slippers: cats

★ Algonquin: the White House-visiting pony

★ Emily Spinach: Alice's pet garden snake, named after an aunt

★ Quentin's miscellaneous snakes, which made appearances at cabinet meetings

★ Leo: Alice's dog, who competed for attention with Jack, Skip, and Sailor Boy, the other resident canines

★ Eli Yale: Theodore Jr.'s pet macaw

★ Bill: a horned toad

★ One kangaroo rat: usually seen in Archie's pocket

★ One black bear

The Roosevelt White House also crawled with lizards and guinea pigs, turtles, hens, and rabbits. More exotic animals were, however, sent to the National Zoo.

Long before there was a National Zoo, **John Quincy Adams** (1825–1829) wasn't sure what to do when his old friend the Marquis de Lafayette came to visit, complete

with alligator. Even a very old friend might be pushing hospitality when he moves in for a few months with such a creature. But Lafayette was a special case, and he received special attention.

Thirty-six towns in the United States carry the name

of the Marquis de Lafayette. So do eighteen counties, countless streets, and one college. The park across the street from the White House is named Lafayette Square. Who was this gentleman, and what was he doing keeping an alligator in the White House?

As a young man of nineteen, Lafayette came to America from France to offer his help in our Revolution. He became a close friend of George Washington. As a general he served at Valley Forge and on other battlefields. He went home to France to fight in his own country's revolution, but was never forgotten for helping Americans in their time of need.

When he was an old man, Lafayette returned to the United States for a final visit. He expected to make a quiet tour, meeting with good friends. Instead, he was greeted as a conquering hero.

From 1825 to 1826 the marquis made a triumphal journey across the country, visiting each of the twenty-four states. He crossed the Gulf of Mexico and steamed up the Mississippi Delta to New Orleans. His first welcoming committees in Louisiana were "enormous alligators of a sinister appearance and sluggish gait, attached to the floating trunks of trees."

What could be more natural than giving Lafayette a present of a real live alligator? When he arrived in Washington in the summer of 1826 with his reptile, Lafayette became the first celebrity to stay in the White House. His good friend John Quincy Adams welcomed him—and his alligator—with open arms. The huge East Room became the temporary home of Lafayette's pet. Its corners, floors, and chairs were also packed with all the other presents Lafayette had collected during his trip.

When the day arrived to leave Washington for France, Lafayette knew he'd never again return to his beloved adopted country. The marquis and President Adams embraced each other. Tears ran down their cheeks. They weren't crocodile tears.

Thomas Jefferson (1801–1809) loved his pet mockingbird. Jefferson was lonely pottering around the Executive Mansion he called "big enough for two emperors, one pope, and the grand lama." The bird hopped along behind him up and down the stairs, and took bits of food from his lips. Jefferson taught it to imitate cats and dogs. When the president played his violin, his mockingbird sat on his shoulder, whistling an accompaniment.

Zachary Taylor (1849–1850) brought his campaign horse, Old Whitey, along with him to the White House. Knock-kneed and uncurried, the old horse placidly cropped grass on the front lawn. He also gave rides to admiring neighborhood children. Some of the kids—and other visitors, too—plucked hairs from his tail for good luck. After Taylor's sudden death, Old Whitey followed the president's casket to his funeral. The empty saddle of a lone horse became a symbol for the loss of a great leader.

After Tad Lincoln's Nanny, the best-known presidential goat was **Benjamin Harrison**'s (1889–1893) His Whiskers. His Whiskers pulled a goat cart for Harrison's grandchildren. Baby McKee was happily riding in the cart one day when the goat got a sudden yen to take off for Pennsylvania Avenue. Pretty soon, there was President Harrison himself, in top hat and frock coat, huffing in hot pursuit of the cart and his favorite grandchild!

N early all the White House families kept dairy cows on the grounds for their daily milk. But during World War I, Mrs. Edith Wilson bought a flock of sheep. The sheep grazed on the lawn to save the cost of gardeners. Their wool was auctioned for the benefit of the Red Cross. Mrs. Wilson was quite proud of the $100,000 she made for the war effort with her flock.

Calvin Coolidge's (1923–1929) presidential household was probably the closest to a zoo after Teddy Roosevelt's. It was home to two canaries called Nip and Tuck, several dogs, and Mrs. Coolidge's tame raccoon, Rebecca. Rebecca even had her own little outdoor house built for her, although she preferred spending her days inside the White House with the president.

Mr. Coolidge's heart, however, belonged to the alley cat Tiger, who'd adopted him on the White House grounds. Tiger joined him at meals. During one political breakfast, Coolidge carefully poured his coffee and cream into a saucer. His guests politely copied him. They waited for the president to take the first sip. Instead, he smiled and put the saucer on the floor for the alley cat. His guests were dumbstruck, but Coolidge didn't care.

Tiger's charms were so great that when the cat strayed, "Silent Cal" got on the radio to ask for help in finding his pet. Tiger turned up a few blocks away making new friends at the Department of the Navy.

Nearly every animal imaginable has been part of the White House zoo over two centuries. But only one president had a "first fish." When **Ronald Reagan** (1981–1989) was recovering in the hospital from a 1981 assassination attempt, he received many presents. One ten-year-old boy sent him a goldfish packed in a water-filled plastic bag. The fish survived the mail and found a happy home in a tank bearing the presidential seal. What higher honor could any creature, great or small, aspire to?

BACKSTAGE AND IN THE WINGS

Carriages jammed the oval driveway before the North Portico of the White House. Horses nickered and pranced in their harness. On the lawns, elegantly dressed multitudes lined up for their turn at admittance. It was January 1, 1863. Inside the great mansion President Abraham Lincoln and his wife, Mary, awaited their New Year's Reception guests.

Mary Todd Lincoln wore diamonds and a silver silk hoop-skirted dress. Garlands of flowers were woven through her dark hair. She looked lovely, yet she was nervous standing beside her tall, soberly clad husband. This was her first official affair since Willie's death almost a year before. Could she bear to greet the long procession of people? The diplomats and military officers, the members of Congress, the citizens of Washington? They'd all come for the annual reception, yes. But they'd come for something more, too.

This was the day Lincoln was to sign his Emancipation Proclamation, freeing the slaves. Congratulations must be given to the President. Some would voice protests. Mrs. Lincoln knew the proclamation was an act of humanity. She knew her husband needed her moral support. She stiffened her spine, smiled, and began to shake hands. Beside her, the president did the same.

More than three hours later, Mr. Lincoln left the Blue Room to climb the stairs to his second-floor office. Members of his Cabinet were waiting for him. Lincoln sat at his table and the proclamation was laid before him. He dipped a gold pen into his inkwell. As his fingers began to tremble over the paper, he set down the pen to steady his arm. It was almost paralyzed from shaking thousands of hands.

"If my name ever goes into history, it will be for this act," Mr. Lincoln thought aloud. "But if my signature looks nervous, people might say, 'He hesitated.'"

The president took a deep breath and tried again. This time he succeeded. He signed his name with strength, in full: *Abraham Lincoln.* He smiled at the document that would change American history.

"There," he said. "That will do."

Not all New Year's Day receptions at the White House were as dramatic as that of 1863. But the tradition of the receptions—making the president's home open and available to all—was a long one.

John Adams (1797–1801) welcomed his fellow citizens to the brand-new White House for the first time on January 1, 1801. **James Monroe** (1817–1825) welcomed them to the rebuilt mansion on January 1, 1818. Every president through **Herbert Hoover** (1929–1933) held open houses. After a thoroughly exhausting session of New Year's Day public handshaking in 1931, it was Hoover who decided enough was enough. He officially abolished the tradition.

Yet today the White House is more accessible to the public than any official residence in the world. Not everyone can shake the president's hand on the first of the new year, but *anyone* can tour the White House. Over *six thousand* visitors a day do this. They do this because they are curious. And there's a lot to be curious about.

The White House has 6 floors, 132 rooms, 32 bathrooms, 147 windows, 412 doors, 12 chimneys, 7 staircases, and 3 elevators. The daily visitors only get to see the formal rooms on the ceremonial floor. The second and third floors are for the private use of the president and his family. The basements are also kept private for security and so that the White House staff can get some work done.

There have always been helpers behind the scenes at the Executive Mansion. When **George Washington** (1789–1797) became president in 1789, he was given a salary of $25,000 a year. This was intended to cover all of his expenses for rent, furnishings, clothing, food, and entertaining. His wife, Martha, brought a few personal servants to New York from Mount Vernon, and they were in business.

Bill Clinton (1993–2001) received an annual salary of $200,000, and after 2001, new presidents will receive $400,000. But now Congress allocates almost $8 million each year to pay for the Executive Mansion's entertaining, maintenance, and service staff of over ninety people. Things have changed since Washington was president. It takes a lot more money and a lot more people to run the White House today.

The mastermind behind all of these helpers is called the Chief Usher. The Chief Usher got his name in the old days, when presidents kept their office on the second floor of the White House. The Chief Usher's job then was to escort, or *usher*, guests upstairs to the president. Today this gentleman is the General Manager of the Executive Mansion. He's in charge of the staff of ushers, butlers, housekeepers, maids, chefs, cooks, doormen, housemen, florists, gardeners, electricians, painters, carpenters, plumbers, storekeepers, and engineers who keep everything running smoothly so that the president can do *his* job.

An army of housemen buff the floors and roll back the rugs after tourists leave each day. A man is employed whose only job is to wash windows and clean the East Room's three fantastic chandeliers. The White House has a laundry in the basement that's run late into the night. The antique furniture is polished daily. There's a florist shop so that the mansion can have fresh flowers. (Mamie Eisenhower loved carnations, and flooded the house with them, the pinker the better. Jacqueline Kennedy preferred more natural flower arrangements. The florist shop restocked with tulips and wildflowers.)

And then there are the plumbers.

Plumbing has been a particular problem at the White House. There's always been water *around* the mansion, and quite often some dripping through a leaky roof. During heavy rains the floors of the kitchens and cellars often were flooded. But there's rarely been enough clean water in the building to *use*.

It seems the piece of land George Washington chose for the Executive Mansion had a nice view—but it was also smack in the middle of a swamp.

In the early years, Tiber Creek ran through the rear of the marshy White House grounds down to the Potomac River. In 1817 the stream was channeled into a canal. It was a sluggish waterway soon filled with sewage, garbage, and dead animals. Mosquitoes and flies infested it—and the nearby White House. Inside the mansion's damp stone walls, the early presidents and their families sometimes choked for breath. The relatives of many presidents complained that they got sick in the White House. They weren't the only ones.

Andrew Jackson (1829–1837) had tuberculosis, and his cough was particularly bad while he lived there.

William Henry Harrison (1841) refused to wear a coat and hat at his inauguration and caught pneumonia giving his speech in the cold rain. His health got worse in the damp and drafty building and he died after only one month in office.

Although some say **Zachary Taylor** (1849–1850) died of eating too many cold cherries and cream in Washington's July heat, more likely it was from typhoid—probably caused by the terrible White House plumbing, or at least the polluted water that ran through it.

Presidents soon learned to leave the malarial grounds of the White House for the summer. **Abraham Lincoln** (1861–1865) packed his family off to the Soldiers' Home three miles away. His secretary, left behind, complained, "I am alone in the White pesthouse. The ghosts of twenty thousand drowned cats come in at night through the south windows."

It wasn't until 1872, during the term of **Ulysses S. Grant** (1869–1877), that the unsanitary Tiber Canal was covered over to make Constitution Avenue. Landscaping was begun to create the mosquito-free Ellipse that is south of the White House today. But even after the swamp was conquered, even after civilized plumbing and clean water existed, the White House was still creating challenges for its plumbers. Only now, the challenges were coming from the presidents themselves.

William Howard Taft (1909–1913) was a portly gentleman. *Portly,* in more polite times, was another word for quite fat. He was our largest president. Taft had presence and a magnificent blond handlebar mustache. He also weighed almost three hundred and fifty pounds. In times of stress, when his presidential reforms were not working as well as he'd like, he gained weight, becoming even larger.

Taft's size created a distinct problem. He overwhelmed the White House bathtubs. After becoming stuck more than once during his bath, Mr. Taft ordered a tub to fit a man of his prominence. Plumbers scurried to take measurements. A foundry labored to cast a monumental mold. The vast iron and enamel tub finally arrived—and all four plumbers installing it fit inside! When they climbed out, Mr. Taft fit inside, too.

A household staff of close to a hundred seems like a lot of people to make a president's life more comfortable in the White House. But a president has access to many more people, not even beginning to count his political team.

The National Park Service uses forty-one employees to care for the fifty-five acres of the president's park surrounding the White House. This includes looking after Lafayette Square, the White House Visitor Center, and the National Christmas Tree on the Ellipse.

The Marine Orchestra of twenty-two members is always at the president's disposal. These are the musicians who play "Hail to the Chief" each time the president and his wife walk down the grand staircase to greet their special guests.

Many of the president's other helpers are invisible—or nearly so. These are the members of his security force, the Secret Service. Early presidents didn't spend much time worrying about their personal security. What they did worry about was keeping state secrets secure.

Thomas Jefferson (1801–1809) invented revolving trays now called "lazy Susans" and had them installed in the walls of his personal dining room. If the servants were kept to the pantry, he reasoned, they wouldn't be hovering around Jefferson's dining table, quietly eavesdropping. Visiting foreign ministers appreciated the delicacy of this arrangement. They were much more willing to speak their minds. Critical negotiations were accomplished without fear of spies.

The second floor Treaty Room adjoined the president's office during the administrations of **William Henry Harrison** (1841) and **John Tyler** (1841–1845.)

Whenever a Cabinet meeting was held there, the door was locked. So why were secret talks being reported in Washington newspapers? Secretary of State Daniel Webster tore out his hair over the problem. Then one day he stepped into the Oval Room next door to find a book. Coming clearly through the wall were the voices of the president and his Cabinet! The first "leak" was discovered. After that, both rooms were locked from the casual visitors strolling the White House hallways.

The Secret Service itself wasn't formed until 1865. It was part of the Treasury Department and its first job was to track down counterfeiters who'd been making a lot of money during the Civil War. Only after **William McKinley**'s (1897–1901) assassination were these officers brought in to watch over the president. By this time there'd been three assassinations of presidents in less than forty years. The public was becoming upset and wanted some action taken.

At first, these special guards were called the White House Police and were only responsible for the president himself. Today the Secret Service guards the president and vice president, their families, and presidential candidates, too.

Naturally, this means the Secret Service must guard the White House, as well. Planes have been flown onto the White House grounds. Guns have been waved before the main gates. More often, though, the very walls of the White House have been surrounded and besieged by pickets. These are people who protest laws that have been made for the country—or even unpopular wars, like the conflict in Vietnam. A president might tire of seeing these folks carrying signs and marching around his house, but he can't do anything about it. Legitimate protest is a very important part of Americans' rights to freedom of speech.

The very first protesters outside the White House were women! In 1917 **Woodrow Wilson** (1913–1921) was deeply involved in trying to fight World War I— and make a lasting peace in the world. *Suffragists* were women who were fighting another war—for the right of all women to vote. What better way to catch the president's attention than to stand outside his house with banners explaining their mission? Mr. Wilson promptly had the women arrested.

But the point was made. After World War I, women were given the vote. They accomplished something else in the process. Because of the suffragists, protesters for many causes learned how to use Pennsylvania Avenue in front of the White House. They learned to use Lafayette Square across the street. The president's front yard became a living billboard of the country's thinking, reasonable or unreasonable.

Of course, the Secret Service had to keep an eye on all these protestors. They also had to continue watching over the presidents. Sometimes the guards' diligence could become overwhelming. Even Theodore Roosevelt called his protectors "a very small but very necessary thorn in the flesh." For older first kids it was worse than that.

🏴 Margaret Truman found that her Secret Service escort made dating nearly impossible. "Consider the effect of saying good night to a boy . . . in a blaze of floodlights, with a Secret Service man in attendance. There is not much you can do except shake hands, and that's no way to get engaged."

🏴 **Lyndon B. Johnson**'s (1963–1969) daughter Luci teased her guardians unmercifully. She also sneaked away from them as often as possible to be alone with her boyfriend. Once she'd decided to get married, though, the Secret Service came in handy. Luci wanted her wedding gown to be a state secret. One of her guards met the gown's designer at the plane and saw that the big gown box was hand-carried into the White House and locked in the Lincoln Bedroom. When Luci posed for her wedding photograph in the East Room before the ceremony, the Secret Service made the entire area off-limits to the house staff—and the bride's fiancé. Luci Johnson had learned to use her protectors.

The Secret Service is also in charge of inaugurations. Bomb-sniffing dogs are walked along the parade routes. Sewers are inspected and manholes are bolted shut. Every precaution is taken for the security of the new president.

Ronald Reagan (1981–1989) didn't want to forget his former movie star days. When he decided to ride his favorite horse from his inauguration cere- monies at the Capitol to the White House, the Secret Service had a fit. A lone man on a horse seemed like a perfect target to them. Still, if a president cannot be reasoned with, he must be accommodated. By the time Mr. Reagan finally changed his mind, the Secret Service had already designed bulletproof long johns and a steel-lined cowboy hat for the president's protection.

While the Secret Service is dealing with the world outside during Inauguration Day, what about the White House staff left behind?

They are having their busiest day in four (or eight) years. The outgoing president is still president until the very moment the oath of office is given to the new leader. The White House staff must wait till that moment. Then they signal the waiting moving vans. The staff has two hours to carry all the belongings of the former president out of the mansion. In the same two hours, they must transfer the incoming president's things. The carpenters hang pictures. The maids refill closets with clothing. A new boss is coming aboard.

The same old White House—and its staff—will welcome him. The residents may change, but the White House remains the same. And on the morning after Inauguration Day, visitors may walk through the White House once more.

It's natural that everyone wants to see it. American history is bound together with this building. It's *our* house, too.

TIMELINE
1797–1885

1789

John Adams
Born: Massachusetts
1797–1801

James Madison
Born: Virginia
1809–1817

George Washington
Born: Virginia
1789–1797

Thomas Jefferson
Born: Virginia
1801–1809

1837

William Henry Harrison
Born: Virginia
1841–1841

James K. Polk
Born: North Carolina
1845–1849

Martin Van Buren
Born: New York
1837–1841

John Tyler
Born: Virginia
1841–1845

1857

Abraham Lincoln
Born: Kentucky
1861–1865

Ulysses S. Grant
Born: Ohio
1869–1877

James Buchanan
Born: Pennsylvania
1857–1861

Andrew Johnson
Born: North Carolina
1865–1869

John Quincy Adams
Born: Massachusetts
1825–1829

James Monroe
Born: Virginia
1817–1825

Andrew Jackson
Born: South Carolina
1829–1837

Millard Filmore
Born: New York
1850–1853

Zachary Taylor
Born: Virginia
1849–1850

Franklin Pierce
Born: New Hampshire
1853–1857

HELLO?
HELLO?

James A. Garfield
Born: Ohio
1881–1881

Rutherford B. Hayes
Born: Ohio
1877–1881

Chester A. Arthur
Born: Vermont
1881–1885

TIMELINE
1885–2001

★ ★ ★

1885

Benjamin Harrison
Born: Ohio
1889–1893

William McKinley
Born: Ohio
1897–1901

Grover Cleveland
Born: New Jersey
1885–1889

Grover Cleveland
Born: New Jersey
1893–1897

1921

Calvin Coolidge
Born: Vermont
1923–1929

Franklin D. Roosevelt
Born: New York
1933–1945

Warren G. Harding
Born: Ohio
1921–1923

Herbert Hoover
Born: Iowa
1929–1933

1963

Richard M. Nixon
Born: California
1969–1974

Jimmy Carter
Born: Georgia
1977–1981

Lyndon B. Johnson
Born: Texas
1963–1969

Gerald R. Ford
Born: Nebraska
1974–1977

William H. Taft
Born: Ohio
1909–1913

Theodore Roosevelt
Born: New York
1901–1909

Woodrow Wilson
Born: Virginia
1913–1921

Dwight D. Eisenhower
Born: Texas
1953–1961

Harry S Truman
Born: Missouri
1945–1953

John F. Kennedy
Born: Massachusetts
1961–1963

George H. W. Bush
Born: Massachusetts
1989–1993

Ronald Reagan
Born: Illinois
1981–1989

Bill Clinton
Born: Arkansas
1993–2001

BIBLIOGRAPHY

Adams, Charles Francis, editor. *Memoirs of John Quincy Adams*. vol. 7. Freeport, N.Y.: Books for Libraries Press, 1969.

Alexander, John. *Ghosts: Washington's Most Famous Ghost Stories*. Arlington, Va.: WBT, 1988.

Bauer, Stephen M., with Leighton, Frances Spatz. *At Ease in the White House: The Uninhibited Memoirs of a Presidential Social Aide*. New York: Carol Publishing Group, 1991.

Blue, Rose, and Corinne J. Naden. *The White House Kids*. Brookfield, Conn.: Millbrook Press, 1995.

Boller, Paul F., Jr. *Presidential Anecdotes*. New York: Penguin, 1982.

Bourne, Miriam Anne. *White House Children*. New York: Derrydale Books, 1985.

Brooks, Noah, edited by Mitgang, Herbert. *Washington in Lincoln's Time*. New York: Rinehart & Company, 1958.

Bryant, Traphes, with Frances Spatz Leighton. *Dog Days at the White House: The Outrageous Memoirs of the Presidential Kennel Keeper*. New York: Macmillan, 1975.

Eaton, Seymour. *The Roosevelt Bears: Their Travels and Adventures*. New York: Dover, 1979 (reprint of 1906 original).

Ewing, Charles. *Yesterday's Washington, D.C.* Miami, Fla.: E. A. Seemann Publishing, 1976.

Fisher, Leonard Everett. *The White House*. New York: Holiday House, 1989.

Hay, Peter. *All the Presidents' Ladies: Anecdotes of the Women Behind the*

Men in the White House. New York: Viking, 1988.

Holzer, Hans. *The Ghosts That Walk in Washington.* Garden City, N.Y.: Doubleday & Company, 1971.

Hunt, Eugenia Jones. *My Personal Recollections of Abraham and Mary Todd Lincoln.* Peoria, Ill.: Helen A. Moser, 1966.

Jensen, Amy La Follette. *The White House and Its Thirty-four Families.* New York: McGraw Hill, 1965.

Johnson, Lady Bird. *A White House Diary.* New York: Dell, 1970.

Levasseur, A. *Lafayette in America in 1824 and 1825; or, Journal of a Voyage to the United States.* Philadelphia: Carey and Lea, 1829.

Means, Marianne. *The Woman in the White House: The Lives, Times and Influence of Twelve Notable First Ladies.* New York: Random House, 1963.

Morris, Edmund. *The Rise of Theodore Roosevelt.* New York: Ballantine, 1980.

Parton, James, edited by Robert V. Remini. *The Presidency of Andrew Jackson.* New York: Harper and Row, 1967.

Quiri, Patricia Ryon. *The White House.* New York: Franklin Watts, 1996.

Seale, William. *The President's House: A History.* 2 vols. Washington, D.C.: White House Historical Association/National Geographic Society, 1986.

Seale, William. *The White House: The History of an American Idea.* Washington, D.C.: American Institute of Architects Press/White House Historical Association, 1992.

Singleton, Esther. *The Story of the White House.* vol 1. New York: Benjamin Blom, 1907.

Smith, Marie. *Entertaining in the White House.* Washington, D.C.: Acropolis Books, 1967.

Smith, Marie, and Louise Durbin. *White House Brides*. Washington, D.C.: Acropolis Books, 1966.

Stamm, Eunice R. *The History of Cheese Making in New York State*. Endicott, N.Y.: Lewis Group Ltd., 1991.

Sullivan, George. *How the White House Really Works*. New York: Lodestar, 1989.

Sullivan, George. *Presidents at Play*. New York: Walker and Company, 1995.

Turner, Justin G. and Linda Levitt Turner. *Mary Todd Lincoln: Her Life and Letters*. New York: Fromm International, 1987.

West, J. B., with Mary Lynn Kotz. *Upstairs at the White House: My Life with the First Ladies*. New York: Coward, McCann & Geoghegan, 1973.

White House Historical Association. *The White House: An Historic Guide*. Washington, D.C.: White House Historical Association, 1995.

Wolff, Perry. *A Tour of the White House with Mrs. John F. Kennedy*. Garden City, N.Y.: Doubleday & Company, 1962.

Worth, Fred L. *Strange and Fascinating Facts about Washington, D.C.* New York: Bell Books, 1988.

For White House Tour Information via the Internet, check:
www.whitehouse.gov

"The White House Is Our House: A CD-ROM Visit," a multimedia cross-platform program, offers users a tour in vivid detail. Produced by Autodesk for The White House Historical Association in cooperation with the American Architectural Foundation.

With thanks to the White House Office of the Archivist and the John F. Kennedy Library for graciously answering reference questions.

INDEX